CENTRAL FLORIDA WRITERS AND PUBLISHERS GUILD

2024 – LET'S GROW TOGETHER

Vision: Purposeful literary expression unfolds through the written and spoken word.

Mission: We are Griots who feed the world with our words.

Key Performance Indicators:

To inspire writers, poets, aspiring and published authors to bring forth their messages.

To assist writers to perfect their craft through public speaking.

To coach members through writers' retreats and workshops.

To showcase authors through promotions, competitions, book signings, and presentations.

To assist authors with the process of publishing their works.

To create space for people to tell their truths.

To encourage writing as part of individual, family, and community legacy.

2025 – WE ARE GRIOTS

MONTHLY ZOOM MEETINGS offer expert speakers on topics promoting the written and spoken word.

ONE-ON-ONE COACHING provides personal assistance to aspiring authors and poets.

WRITE, RIGHT TO THE POINT focuses upon students and adults seeking to improve their writing for specific purposes, such as higher education entrance essays and job/career changes, respectively.

THE FUTURE SPEAKS NOW targets young persons ages 13-25 who seek avenues to let their voices be heard through quality writing and speaking.

THE WRITING ROOM affords spaces where writers can respond to prompts and share their work, offering enhancement critiques.

Become a Member Investor Today!

THE CENTRAL FLORIDA WRITERS AND PUBLISHE
cfwpgi@gmail.com
BUS COMPLETE CHK (...9958)

Zelle

The Central Florida Writers and Publishers Guild, Inc.
$CFWPGGive

Griots and Griottes

In West Africa, its history written in its own languages is relatively new.

African history was written in European languages during the colonial era, and in Arabic for centuries. But well since before that, in communities in the Sahel and Savanna regions, the *griots* (men) and *griottes* (women) have spoken, from memory, epic-long histories and genealogies that often take days to recite.

African "Wordsmiths"

For hundreds of years, possibly beginning before the birth of Christ, the griots and griottes have served as human links between past and present, speaking the stories of their ancestors and the history of their people, all to preserve not just a family or a community but an entire culture and its values.

In Africa, this role, unique to that continent for centuries, now adopted, to various extents, by countries around the world, includes many diverse responsibilities: not just oral historian and genealogist, but also teacher, spokesperson, exhorter, interpreter, poet, storyteller, diplomat, adviser to nobility, family counselor, judge, messenger, master of ceremonies, praise singer, and musician, to name just a few.

Griottes, considered by West Africans as being fundamentally different from all other human beings, are not religious icons, nor are they sorcerers, but they hold an aura of power and mystery that is at once revered and frightening. Nearly omniscient, the wordsmiths can sing ones praises... or ones doom.

http://news.psu.edu/story/140694/2002/05/01/research/keepers-history

Oral Historians

While both roles involve preserving history through oral tradition, a "griot" is a specific West African storyteller, musician, and oral historian who traditionally passes down family and community history through song and narrative, often at important events like weddings, whereas an "oral historian" is a broader term for someone who collects and interprets personal accounts of historical events. through interviews, usually with a focus on documenting a wider range of perspectives and experiences; essentially, a griot is a specialized form of oral historian deeply rooted in West African culture and tradition.

Articles edited

Board of Directors

Dr. Ruth Baskerville, President

Ms. Yolanda Triplett, Vice President

Ms. Marie McKenzie, Secretary

Dr. Free Harris, Treasurer

Mr. Ted Hollins, President Emeritus

Ms. Marcia Williams, President Emeritus

President's Message

Dr. Ruth L. Baskerville

There is an old African Proverb that says, *"When an old man dies, a library burns to the ground."* This is an urgent message to all of us who are blessed to have elders as the matriarchs and patriarchs of our families. We must not let them leave this earth before we write or record their life stories. How many of us have children and grandchildren whose relationships to their grandparents and great-grandparents are limited to pointing at a faded picture of someone whom they never met?

Griots are storytellers who keep their family legacies alive. We are the Griots of this day and at this hour. Just look around to see a room full of aspiring and published authors, editors, publishers, cover designers and illustrators. I'm a ghostwriter, which means that when you have something important to share with an audience but can't find the words to express what's inside of you, your ghostwriter becomes the "midwife" of words to help you "birth out" your book.

I am in awe of God's grace in sending me eighty-one writers for whom I've been editor or ghostwriter, and they are all published authors, some award-winning like me. Best of all, their stories are resonating with folks who glean knowledge, wisdom, and even comfort from reading them.

Today, at the beginning of 2025, why not purpose in your heart to believe that you have a message to convey that your family or the widest audience that social media affords will want to receive? Like the words on your little black book table favors say, you possess "THE POWER OF START."

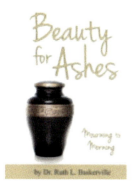

BEAUTY FOR ASHES: Mourning to Morning allows readers to follow Dr. Ruth's life four years after becoming a widow. She has romantic interests, job opportunities, and a life full of joy. Her "new normal" can never replace the exceptional life she lived with her one true love, Waverly Baskerville. However, with the right attitude and a thirst to find God's purpose for her life, she has experienced, as stated in Isaiah 61:3, ""To all who mourn, he will give a crown of beauty for ashes, a joyous blessing instead of mourning."

FINDING HUMOR IN GRIEF is Dr. Ruth Baskerville's sad and funny story of dealing with bereavement after losing her husband of forty-five years. It's a stream-of-consciousness account of personal recovery and spiritual healing, as she found her "new normal." She found bits of humor being a single woman again. Dr. Ruth says, "I've learned that grief is like a roller coaster, where the ride never ends, and the goal is to find the courage to let go your grip of the safety bar and raise your arms high in the air, as you 'free fall' with confidence that you'll land safely, in your right mind."

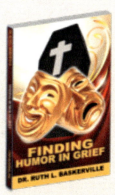

HOODLESS KLAN is the story of a veteran educator who accepted the position of Principal of Pine Woods Charter Elementary School. Dr. Grace Middleton faced a group of manipulative, wealthy racists within the school system who insisted she be complicit in taking unscrupulous actions against minority children and parents. When she refused, they joined forces with key central office personnel to ruin her reputation and fire her. Dr. Grace stood her ground and became the modern-day antidote to the poison of never-ending racism.

Dr. Ruth L. Baskerville

wwexcellence.org   321.247.8591   wrbaskerville@gmail.com

KEYNOTE SPEAKER
Anderson Hill II

Anderson Hill II is a trailblazer in law, business, and community service. A first-generation college graduate, he earned dual degrees in law and business from the University of Florida, later serving as an attorney for the CIA and Bethune-Cookman University. Together with his wife, Sandra, he leads HZ Construction, a family-owned contracting business known for major projects like the KIA Center and public schools in Orange County, Florida.

Married for 47 years, the Hills are parents, grandparents, and soon-to-be great-grandparents, devoted to their faith and community through over 40 years of service as Deacon and Deaconess.

"BLACK PROFESSIONAL LIFE: CONSTANT DRAMA"

Anderson's latest book is a heartfelt tribute to his love affair with Sandra and a continuation of the narrative from his first book published in 1997. This work delves into his relationships—religious, professional, and personal—while highlighting his commitment to service. Anderson has led two impactful non-profits: Education is Cool – Get One, Inc., which has awarded scholarships and provided free construction training courses, and Men of JESUS, Inc., which focuses on guiding men to faith in Jesus Christ.

DOUBLE AGENT: CONVICTED SAINT
Anderson Hill, II
Excerpt

"I was a good man, incapable of a sin so grave that I could come to see myself in jail. I knew the law and belonged to the *Florida Bar Association*. I was even a CIA Agent with a top security clearance. I was a loving father and husband, too. Then, I 'fell from grace.' What happened to me?

The truth is that I have been convicted. I've been drunk on most days -- drunk in my sorrows and drunk in my problems. That's not all. My mind was clouded by drugs, as I had tried to escape the reality of what had so quickly become a miserable life.

I found myself denying the many and complex reasons for my present situation, and it's true that I was scared of facing the consequences of my terribly poor decisions. I had been blinded by the desire to acquire money, and in my quest to have more and more of it, I made the wrong decisions in life, one after the other.

Now, I know the truth, and this book is my journey to hell and then back. Now I know who I am. At the point where I had money without chasing after it, I felt strong and powerful. But money really gave me nothing but false power. I believed the misconception that without money, I would be nothing but a weak man. I was wrong. There came a point where I realized that without my family, I am nothing but a lonely person. Without my faith, I am nothing but a lonely man walking in a desert with no direction in life, just surviving without any forward-moving direction in which to go.

Thankfully, I can say that by God's grace, I still have my family, and I still have my faith. So, all hope is not lost. This time I am stronger. My God has given me a reason to take hold of my life. The *Holy Bible* assures me in Deuteronomy 28:13 (NKJV): *'And the LORD will make you the head and not the tail; you shall be above only, and not be beneath, if you [a]heed the commandments of the LORD your God, which I command you today, and are careful to observe them.'*"

My God has shown me the way to move in the right direction. He has given me signs of where to go, and because I finally hear His voice regularly, here I am ready to trust Him. Now I have the confidence to take the wheel of my life and to go where my God wants to take me. I am ready to take my life back as a *Double Agent: Convicted Saint*.

To get a copy of the book, email your request to
educationiscool5282@gmail.com.

Lavatryce Simpson Singfield
Speaker

Lavatryce Simpson Singfield is the second of seven grandchildren of Waldorf Astor Singfield, Sr. and Lavatryce C. Simpson Singfield, the 2 people who wrote the beautiful letters which comprise her book, *A Legacy of Love.* It is an epistolary memoir written between 1924 and 1926. Lavatryce is her grandmother's namesake. Since childhood she has always loved writing and reading books and was beyond excited when she read the letters that her grandparents had written to each other from the time they met to the day they got married. She was happy when her grandmother gave her an approval to write a book with them.

Ms. Singfield is a graduate of *Howard University*. After graduation she lived and worked in multiple cities in 7 states across the United States while achieving a successful career in the fields of management, individual retirement plans, mortgage underwriting, and healthcare provider credentialing and health insurance enrollment. She is currently retired and owns a house in St. Louis, Missouri and in Hollywood, Florida. She grew up in a very close and happy family surrounded by wonderful family artifacts and photos. Knowledge of ancestors and oral family history have been an important part of her life.

Order using QR code
and $30

Order of the Programme

Welcome, Introductions .... Dr. Ruth Baskerville
       Honorable Orange County Mayor Jerry L. Demings Message

Invocation and Blessing .... Ms. Yolanda Triplett

Brunch Served and Vendor Table Visits .... Ms. Yolanda Triplett

Introduction of Ten Vendors .... Ms. Yolanda Triplett

Introduction of Speaker Ms. Lavatryce Singfield .... Dr. Free Harris

Introduction of Keynote Speaker Mr. Anderson Hill, II .... Dr. Ruth Baskerville

"What You Know and What You *Thought* You Knew" .... Dr. Free Harris

Recognition of Youth Guild Members and Student Attendees .... Dr. Free Harris

Opportunity for Membership, Donations, T-Shirt Purchases .... Dr. Free Harris

Benediction, Closing Prayer .... Mr. Anderson Hill, II

Special Thanks

Honorable Mayor of Orange County, Jerry L. Demings

Orange County Sheriff John Mina

Special Guests

Jenifer Dearinger, President Writers Alliance of Gainesville

Doris Heard, JRM book Club, Mt. Pleasant Church

Erik Deckers, President Writers of Central Florida or Thereabouts

Elyse Jardine, Director Community Outreach United Arts of Central Florida

Charise Liburd, Edyth Bush Foundation's Empowering Good Mentor 2024

Absent: Shawn Welcome, President Next Level Speakers Academy, Orlando Chapter, Poet Laureate The City Beautiful

Brunch Planning Team

Gwen Bennett-Gray

Welton James

Nyah Vanterpool

Vendors

Gwen Bennett-Gray

Denise Bethea-Snell

Dr. Michelle Dunlap

Essex James

Welton James

Donors

Morton Anman, PA

Anderson Hill

James H. Scott

Leticia Lamar

Pamela Marshall-Koons

Akiya Maston

Lavatryce Singfield

Mark and Sharee Thomas

Social Media Influencers

Owen Crosby

Arya Malekjahani

Musicians

Bill Moss, Saxophone

Devrick Bell, Trumpet

Web Master

Sean Lane

Black Books/Pen Table Favors

Gwen Bennett-Gray

Micah Massey

Greeters

Laurae' Williams

LaTonya Grace

Flyer Designer

Gaye Johnson

Programme Journal Layout and Publication

Essex James

Marcia Williams

Caterer

Ms. Robin Cuffie Johnson

Macedonia Missionary Baptist Church, Eatonville, Florida

Orlando Garden Club

Ms. Jeannie Kroemer, Treasurer

Waverly's Way Tutoring

About Dr. Ruth

Founder: Dr. Ruth Baskerville

- Dr. Ruth Baskerville is a veteran educator and administrator of nearly 50 years.
- She's been teacher, principal K – 12, and Central office head of personnel and of curriculum.
- Now retired, Dr. Ruth is CEO and founder of Waverly's Way tutoring from kindergarten to a doctorate, including GED, SAT, State testing, more.

Why Waverly's Way?

- Our tutors will help with homework in grades K-12!
- Prepare for Florida State Assessments (FSA), SAT, ACT, and GED!
- Provides post-secondary and Ph.D. Guidance
- Affordable pricing!
- Fully virtual, no travel is needed!

Register Now

https://www.wwexcellence.org

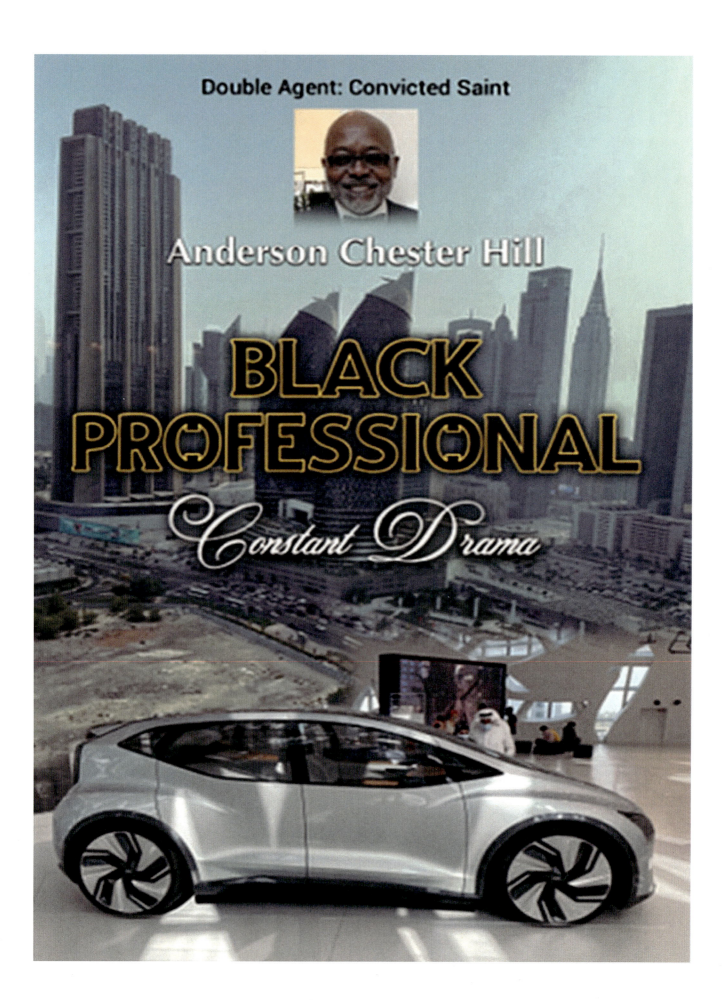

Hey Wonderful!
DR. NANOTCHKA CHUMLEY
BREAST CANCER ADVOCACY COACH

Ask Me About
- I have breast cancer, now what?
- How to navigate your diagnosis
- Understanding your treatment options
- Creating Equity in the healthcare system

About Me

Dr. NaNotchka M. Chumley is the CEO and Founder of the International Patient Advocacy Institute. As a Black female physician, she has helped Black women understand and navigate their breast cancer diagnosis and determine the best option for themselves and their families.

As the #1 best-selling author of *The Best Patient Advocate*. Dr. Chumley uses her body of work to help newly diagnosed breast cancer patients break through the complicated healthcare process and tip the scales in their favor.

Her work as a physician and Breast Cancer Advocacy Coach has gotten her on The Uncontrolled Substance radio show, the Who's Who Top Doctor publication in Los Angeles, and a featured article in Top Doctor in Best in California Magazine.

Dr. Chumley is not shy about going on the record to say, "I treat the patient, not the paper." This motto drives her to get the best outcomes possible for her breast cancer clients.

When NaNotchka is not helping her clients break through the complicated and overwhelming process of their breast cancer diagnosis, she loves to travel, dance, fine dining, and enjoy sunsets at the beach. She lives with her husband in Los Angeles.

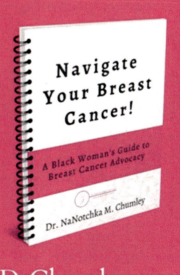

DrChumley.com

INTERNATIONAL PATIENT ADVOCACY INSTITUTE

MARIE MCKENZIE

Award-winning
#1 Bestselling Author

About Marie

Once silenced by the trauma of sexual assault, Marie McKenzie has dedicated her life to breaking the silence surrounding the most underreported crime. She champions survivors and equips healthcare providers with tools to deliver compassionate, trauma-informed care. Her mission is to empower healthcare teams with the knowledge and confidence to support survivors effectively. To further this cause, she founded the Sexual Assault Coaching Institute, a platform for advocacy, education, and transformation in the fight against sexual violence.

With over two and a half decades of experience as a registered nurse, including her role as a sexual assault nurse examiner in the clinical and community settings, Marie blends her professional expertise with the tools and techniques that facilitated her healing journey.

Renowned for her award-winning and bestselling memoir, Things That Keep Me Up At Night, Marie chronicles her odyssey from sexual assault at the age of eleven to her triumphant transformation.

Her book is a beacon of hope, encouraging others to find their voices, share their stories, seek support, and embrace a life imbued with purpose.

Marie doesn't shy away from proudly declaring, "My Mission is to remove sexual assault from being the number one underreported crime in America."

When Marie is not working with women on their journey or educating providers, she collaborates with various organizations dedicated to helping those affected by diverse traumas. She enjoys the vibrant life of Orlando, Florida, alongside her husband, George.

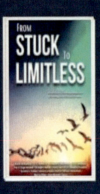

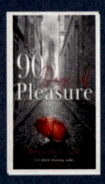

linktr.ee/mckenziemar

SCAN ME

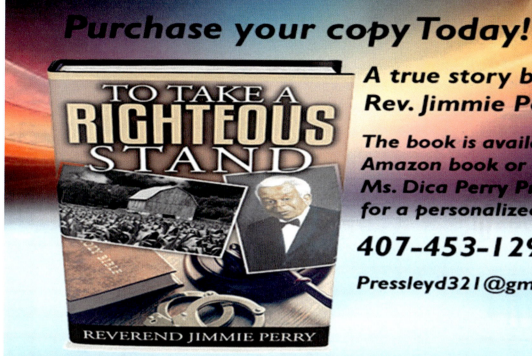

To Take a Righteous Stand is Rev. Jimmie Perry's true story about his grandfather, James Arthur Perry standing alone against the racist community in Dothan, Alabama in 1931. It's about the *Federal Seed & Fertilizer Loan Act of 1930*, the theft of money by corrupt racists, and because Perry didn't get the promised funds, his family lost their 92-acre farm.

When the Government learned of the fraud, it sent U. S. Marshals to Dothan for what became a 4-year trial that was the longest in American history to that point. It was the first time that a Black man testified in a court, and certainly the first time where half the town of White, corrupt men went to jail because of Perry's testimony.

Yes, the Government won its case, but the 92-acre Perry farm was never returned and the family had to flee the KKK by night. James Arthur Perry and many family members started new lives in Orlando, Florida, but every "Perry" left Dothan, Alabama.

This story is about legacy, history, courage, family ties across continents, and triumph because God was in the midst of it all. The family's motto is, '"PERRY PROUD!" The book is available on Amazon, or you may want a personalized copy from Ms. Dica Perry Pressley, the last living child of James Arthur Perry.

407-453-1296

Pressleyd321@gmail.com

Purchase your copy Today!

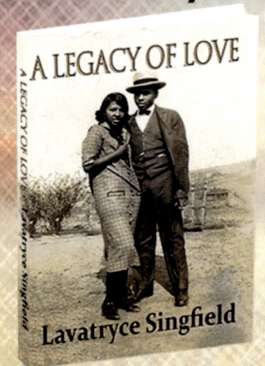

A true love story of Waldorf & Lavatryce Singfield.

The book is available on Amazon book. Contact Lavatryce Singfied for a personalized copy or interview.

authorlavatrycesingfield@yahoo.com

This book tells the love story of Lavatryce Singfied paternal grandparents as told through some actual letters they wrote to each other between 1924 and 1926.

A subsidiary of Jamesce Associates, LLC

Uniquelly Creative

Essex J. James
Creative Designer-Illustrator

creativediga.com
ejcreate@mail.com

P. O. Box 780087
Orlando, FL 32878
tel 813.545.6378

coroflot.com/EssexJames/portfolio

Graphics Design • Children's Illustrations • Logo designs • Animated Videos

1-888-645-0050
WilliamsAndKingPublishers.com

Marcia Williams
President

Bill Moss & Devrick Bell

Trumpet & Saxophone
352-406-4690
billmoss80@live.com

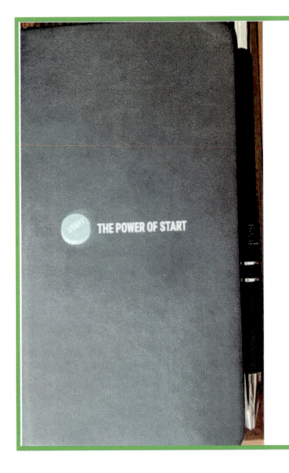

NOBODY TAKES OUR HISTORY

I have donated these small journals to each guest at the Central Florida Writers and Publishers Guild Brunch because, as a Blasian (Black-Asian) woman, published author, and entrepreneur, I recognize that we must claim our truths and then proclaim them to readers and listeners everywhere. You even have a pen, so, start writing!

Gwen Bennett-Gray

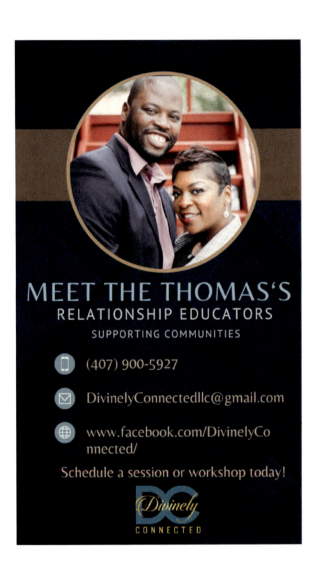

- ACCOMPLISHED AUTHOR
- ENGAGING SPEAKER
- EDUCATOR/ CONSULTANT
- WRITING COACH/ EDITOR
- DIVERSITY-AFFIRMING EVANGELIST
- COMMUNITY INSPIRER

Michelle R. Dunlap, Ph.D.

DrMichelleTeaches.com
drmichelledunlap@yahoo.com
860-608-0084

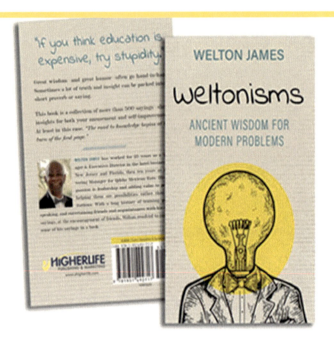

Weltonisms: Ancient Wisdom for Modern Problems, the book to inspire people with advice and wisdom. Welton's goal is to teach people about self-responsibility in a unique way that people can apply to any situation. There are short quips that Welton uses to inspire thousands of people over his 25 years as Manager & Executive Director in the hotel business, and 15 years as Catering Manager & Director of Leadership for Qdoba Mexican Eats. Welton believes that people need to be encouraged, inspired, helped to see possibilities rather than limitations. **Need a speaker, contact Welton James at 407-592-6983 or welton@weltonjames.com.**

Nikki Giovanni speaks on "Writing"

"We write because we believe the human spirit cannot be tamed and should not be trained."

DENISE BETHEA-SNELL
Founder & CEO

📞 407-710-5612

🌐 www.womenwitharighteouscry.org

✉️ righteouscry@ymail.com

FOLLOW US

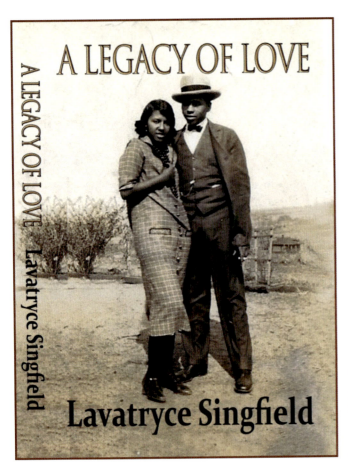

We Are Ventura Leadership Solutions

Supporting leaders in achieving what matters the most in life.

Career & Ministry Solutions Here

Executing your dreams and empowering those you lead to do the same, requires prescribed achievement. Let us assist.

Why Choose Us

+ Career & Industry Certification Specialist, Youth Ministry Liaison
+ Transformational Life Coaching

Innovative
Advanced mind mapping to chart your pathway to success.

Collabrative
Your "Vision" and our years of expertise produces reality.

Solutions Minded
We promote a holistic approach to achievement-- body, soul, spirit.

Contact Now

352.462.2804

leticia@venturaleadershipsolutions.com

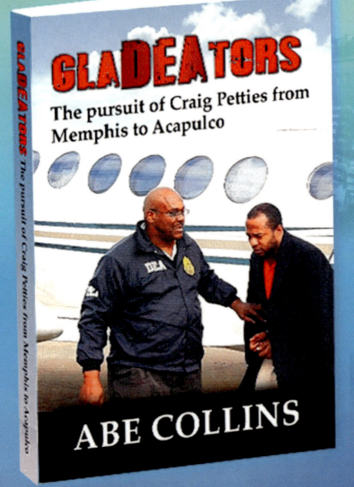
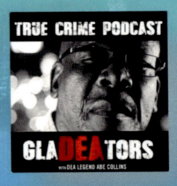

True Crime
★ ★ ★ ★
Listen on Apple Podcasts

Purchase your copy Today!

Scan to purchase your copy at Amazon.com

Contact Abe Collins to get your personal sign copy:

Abe Collins

407 572-2696

collinsabe4@gmail.com

Deagladeators.com

Made in the USA
Middletown, DE
31 January 2025

70597267R00018